This edition published by Kids Can Press in 2017

Originally published in French under the title *Les vacances de facteur souris* by Les Éditions Casterman s.a.

© 2016 Casterman
Text and illustrations by Marianne Dubuc

English translation © 2017 Kids Can Press
English translation by Yvette Ghione

Kids Can Press gratefully acknowledges the financial support of the Government of Ontario, through the Ontario Media Development Corporation; the Ontario Arts Council; the Canada Council for the Arts; and the Government of Canada, through the CBF, for our publishing activity.

Published in Canada and the U.S. by Kids Can Press Ltd.
25 Dockside Drive, Toronto, ON M5A 0B5

Kids Can Press is a Corus Entertainment Inc. company

www.kidscanpress.com

The text is set in Gill Sans.

English edition edited by Yvette Ghione
Printed and bound in Shenzhen, China, in 7/2016 by C & C Offset

CM 17 0 9 8 7 6 5 4 3 2 1

Library and Archives Canada Cataloguing in Publication

Dubuc, Marianne, 1980–
[Vacances de facteur souris. English]
   Mr. Postmouse takes a trip / written and illustrated by Marianne Dubuc.

Translation of: Les vacances de facteur souris.

ISBN 978-1-77138-354-7 (hardback)

   I. Title. II. Title: Vacances de facteur souris. English.

PS8607.U2245V3313 2017   jC843'.6   C2016-902317-6

Mr. Postmouse
Takes a Trip

MARIANNE DUBUC

Mr. Postmouse   Mrs. Mouse   Pip   Milo   Lulu

Kids Can Press

Hooray for vacation! The post office is closed, and Mr. Postmouse is setting off on a trip with his family.

He's bringing along a few parcels for delivery — a postmouse's rounds are never done!

"See you soon, Milo! Goodbye, Lulu! Bye, Pip!" Mr. Bear says to the mouselings.

First stop: the forest. The Mouse family visits Aunt Claudette, who lives in a cute little camper. Mr. Postmouse has a special delivery for her, of course!

Milo sets up the tent while
Mrs. Mouse stokes the
cooking fire for lunch.

Next, there's nothing like a day at the beach! Lulu builds a castle for Mr. Crab.

And Pip is concentrating so hard on keeping his kite in the air that he doesn't even notice the ice-cream truck!

The adventure continues at sea aboard the *Rosetta*, a cruise ship famous for its opera performances and five-star restaurant.

Careful, Milo! The sea
is full of surprises!

Then, ashore on a volcanic island, Mr. Postmouse makes a delivery to Tarzan before stopping by his friend Mr. Dragon's summer home for a visit.

"Mmmm! Volcano-roasted marshmallows!" That Milo is always peckish.

Their trek leads the Mouse family
into the desert on camelback. It's
scorching hot!

Beside an oasis, Mr. Postmouse sets up
the cooking pot while Mrs. Mouse brings
Mr. Lizard a mysterious envelope ...

In the heart of the jungle, Mr. Postmouse and the mouselings are on a photo safari. Mind the roaming tigers!

LOULOU

Mrs. Mouse delivers a package
to a delighted Mrs. Winks.

And then it's a quick city stop!
"Here's a pot of honey from your
cousin Mr. Bear!" says Milo to the
other Mr. Bear.

SWEETS

Mr. Postmouse enjoys a taste of Jake's cakes. But where has Pip scurried off to?

After the hustle and bustle of the city, a relaxed mountain picnic is just the thing!

The Marmots offer Lulu a cookie to thank her for bringing them their important parcel: bright and woolly winter socks!

From the mountains to an ice field!
The Mouse family will spend the night in
the cozy igloo Mrs. Mouse is building.

Brrr! Mr. Postmouse is happy to warm up at Mr. Polar Bear's with a cup of tea.

Everyone takes to the skies to make one last delivery.

Milo tests his jet pack. *Zoom!* He's off like a rocket.

Pip prefers to travel by duck.

Their vacation over, the Mouse family arrives home with a suitcase full of souvenirs from their amazing trip.

Oh, dear! Letters have piled up at the post office. It looks like Mr. Postmouse will be off on his rounds again tomorrow!